Shreds of thoughts -
Gedankenfetzen

Astrid Evelt

Shreds of thoughts -
Gedankenfetzen

Bibliografische Information der Deutschen Nationalbibliothek:
Die Deutsche Nationalbibliothek verzeichnet diese Publikation in der Deutschen
Nationalbibliografie; detaillierte bibliografische Daten sind im Internet
über http://dnb.d-nb.de abrufbar

Herstellung und Verlag: BoD - Books on Demand GmbH, Norderstedt

ISBN: 9783732236749

Vorwort oder so etwas

Eines vorne weg, dieses Buch habe ich erstmal für
mich kreiert und da finden sich eben Sachen wieder,
die ich geschrieben habe und die ich gut finde, ob
ihr als Leser das auch so seht, überlasse ich euch.

Hier sind so einige Blogeinträge von mir und andere
schräge Gedanken und ein paar Kommentare dazu
zusammen gefasst. Einige Sachen kann man auch
online finden, aber dafür muss man lange suchen.
Zeitlich sind sie nicht unbedingt geordnet und manches
ist auch überarbeitet worden und manches ist nicht mal
beendet - und das mit Absicht.
Diese Gedanken umspannen einen Zeitrahmen von
über 20 Jahren und einige ähneln sich. Manches
betrifft mich selbst,
manches habe ich für andere geschrieben und manches
spiegelt einfach nur ein Gefühl wieder. Der
überwiegend Teil der Einträge ist englisch, aber es sind
natürlich auch deutsches Material mit dabei...

 Ich habe alles frei nach meinem Gutdünken gemacht
und es in die Form gefasst, die mir zusagt und das
Ganze als das bezeichnet, was es ist: Gedankenfetzen!
Die kann nicht jeder verstehen oder nachvollziehen oder
auch nicht jeder mögen, aber das muss man auch nicht.
Das Ganze hat keinerlei Ansprüche und muss auch nicht
in irgendeinem Literaturkurs gelesen werden, also ihr
entscheidet, ob ihr euch das antut oder nicht!
Also, wünsche ich euch gutes Durchkommen durch
den Dschungel der Gedanken und Gefühle...

Astrid aka WolfEmpress

Sometimes there's a love like no other
someone you can hold on to
someone you can trust
someone you can believe in
someone who's always there for you
no matter what

You never know
what you did to deserve this
when you always believed
yourself to be the devil
never seeing the gentle hero inside
with a soft soul
which can be broken easily
by the foolish and angry words
of another broken soul

You thought you lost it all
But it's all there,
the love, the strength, the energy,
the warmth and happiness
If you see past the outside image
there's the truth inside of you
You know what you want
and you know what to do
You know what's worth to fight for

No one can tell you
what to do
it's all up to you
sometimes you need
to read between the lines
to know what's right
Listen to your heart and
follow the song of love
You can find the answer
in the eyes where
all of that is mirrored
You see the love shines back to you

Someone, who loves you no matter
what
Break down the walls around
your heart and soul
built up through anger, hurt and grief
and let that love shine into it all
Love is stronger than this
and you can believe in this love

Love

1. When I first heard of you
I didn't believe that
you'd be the one to love me
I know that
you can see me as I am
Your love is bigger
than any rational thought
Your love's deeper than
the eyes can see

It's even there
When I try to fight it
Loving you wasn't
always easy for me
Feeling like climbing
over mountains and
swimming through
oceans to get to you
I never knew

You were there with me
You're always
by my side
overcoming all
obstacles in my way
When I stumble and fall
you lift me up
With you I feel like
my soul soars above the stars

Refrain:
I live contentedly
in your warmth and safety

You give me strength on my way
no matter where I am
no matter what I do

You're there with me
 Even if I can't see you
with my eyes
I can feel your nearness
beside me and
your presence and love deep down inside me
in my mind, heart and soul
My heart is your home

2. When I lose my mind

Going in circles
I turn around
I can see your radiance shines unto me
in the darkest night
You always believe in me against all odds
With you by my side I smile wider
I can breathe again
I think in better ways
making the world a colourful place
Love is your answer to
the cries of my soul

3.

And even if I lose my voice
My heart always sings your words
I can hear your voice everywhere
You're the first thing on my mind
and you're the last
You'll be there, when I'm gone

I can trust you now
When I have to find the way
through the mist
of confusion and depression
into the light to be with you

Wherever you are is my home
Where it's safe for me to say
I love you

Gedankenfetzen

Wenn die sanften Helden ihre Ruhmeshalle kriegen, sind die
Meisten begeistert, nur nicht die verlorenen Furien

Sie schreien nach Vergeltung für die große Liebe, die ihnen
verwährt wurde
Sie scheitern an der Magie ihrer eigenen Worten und
zerbrechen an dem Zauber, den sie gesprochen haben, um
die Gerechtigkeit zu bekommen -

Denn Gerechtigkeit lässt sich nicht erzwingen.

Magic Love

f - first vocal; s - second vocal, ()- background
vocals

f&s Intro
Have I ever seen the sun
shining through your heart?
Do I really feel this for you or
is it just a mirror of my fantasy?

1. f) I can't believe it,
you've hidden your feelings before
At last you're next to me,
love's shining through it all
You call out my name
and it sings in my ears
Love flows right into my heart

f&s
Come on, I wanna hold you forever
Lifted to seventh heaven
with every touch
We had to be strong to get so far
This seemed like a dream before
(Finally it's all true)
Let's get together in this harmony

Chorus
f&s So, reach out for this love
Together we can touch the stars
Sweet flames burn out of dreams
(Just like this, dreams come true)
It's like magic love
the bound between you and me
Oh, magic love
that keeps me by your side

2. s) I felt down, 'cause I couldn't be with you
My history tore us apart and
it was a long way to get back here,
this time we can face it together
You stand by my side,
when I'm feeling bad
You're my sun, with you
I can feel my world coming alive

f&s
Come on, I wanna..

Chorus
f&s So, reach out for this love...

12 Songs for "Within or Without You"

1. My Night

Welcome to this world of darkness
This is the kind of blackness, in
Which borders can't be traced
You don't know, who you are
You don't know, where you are
There's no beginning
There's no end
Just the darkness
to engulf your senses

Welcome to my night
A world, where the mind is drowned
In an endless nightmare
My night never ends
When you open your eyes
You will not see
If you look for love
You will not find
Trapped in my night
There's no escape
There's nowhere to run to,
Because there's no way out

If you feel alone
You find no relief
You can find no one
In this dark place
It drives you crazy
And nobody hear your cries
For the darkness swallows them all
If you try to think sane
You will fail
Because the blackness
Devours them all with insanity

2. Understanding

I thought I was the next one
The next one in line
I ought to go
I shouldn't linger here
Why did you have to go?
And leave me here alone
I feel out of place
No one to teach me
The ways of life
I couldn't tie
My shoes without you
No one here to make me smile

There's no feel of understanding
Everything's out of reach
Breaking of dawn makes me sad
Why am I here?
Why must I linger?
This makes no sense
What is the greater good
You've been sacrificed to?
I don't understand it all

They say it all will be good
Some day and someplace
It won't hurt anymore
But who are they to tell me
How I feel about life?

I tried to change it all around,
But I still sit
In the same old house,
Doing the same old things
Without you
I want to cry right now
I want to die right now
Where's the sense in that?

3. Hell's fire or Heaven's delight

Hell's fire or Heaven's delight
When you cannot tell what's what
You're on a rollercoaster
That puts your feelings
In a constant limbo
You don't know,
If your life's going up or down

When heaven feels like hell,
Love and hate have
No significance
All deems a faded vision
Friends and lovers only
Cause you pain,
When heaven feels like hell
When you have no idea,
Where your emotions might go
You're stuck between

Hell's fire and Heaven's delight
It feels warm like the sunlight
And burning like a flame
At the same time
You cannot turn around
You cannot run away
It brings you light and doom
No matter what
You will be the master
You will be the subject
You love and fear it
Because it's like a blaze
Of sensations

No one can tell you
What is the right path
It's up to you, whether this is
Hell's fire or Heaven's delight

Either your will
Brings you through the
Emotional thunderstorm
And makes you stronger
Or you face your own hell
Now you decide
Choose well
This might be the only chance
To see Hell's Fire or Heaven's delight

4. The Queen of Ice

Feel the chill of her words
Sending ice through your veins
See her cold smile
That freezes hell over
The Queen of Ice is in charge

And your senses turn around
Her eyes bear you down
The frosty fury makes you weak
She acts friendly, but never
Really shows sympathy
Wherever she walks
The Nordic wind is not far behind
The Queen of Ice is in charge

Her attitude is like the snow
Beautiful, silent, inviting,
But deathly if you remain too long
You see her charming ways
You'll be wrapped around her finger
Within the blink of an eye
The world grows colder then
The Queen of Ice is in charge

5. Walk the Line

It's hard to walk the line that
Either creates chaos in your life
Or brings you eternal peace
You cannot see the passage
In the mists of life
You have to trust
Your gut instincts

It's hard to walk the line
When voices call out to you
Asking you to come
Confusing you
Disappoint you
Crying for you
You can hear them in the mist
Reaching out for you
With their own needs

One step after another
Don't try to falter
Oh, I know how hard it is
To walk the line
Without seeing the goal
You want to reach
Without seeing the traps
On the way
Just keep on walking,
Because in the end
It's all we can do

6. Face my life

In the end of the day
I face myself
What do I see in
The lines of my eyes?
Where's the love's smile?
All I can see is
The ashes of destruction
In my eyes

It's no big drama
That I had to face in my life
Little pain can craft
Great chaos in the end
All the lying, luring,
Deceiving and hurting
Drive my senses low
I'm standing on the edge
And taking a leap of faith
Is a risk and it's
Not appealing at all

It's hard to stand up
For your dreams
When they're washed out
I even don't recall
The day they faded away
Away into dull nothingness
There's not much I can do

A little interlude (No song)
and a love letter to anyone (This is fiction;
I just needed to write this down)

Hello my darling,
as I told you many times before -
I love you.
Yet you seem to believe that I don't
mean them, you look and smile to me,
without looking at me.
Don't you know that it hurts?!
I told I'm here for you.
My arms are open for you -
I try to let and keep you in my world.

You're the only one I opened
this door for, but you seem to ran past it.
Can't you see, there's no one else?
And never will be.
You let me down so many times before -
without knowing it.
I've forgiven you,
my love is stronger than that.
If you need someone to love,
someone to run to,
someone to understand,
someone to care.. I am here.
Ciao, me

7. Hungry Ghosts

Your life hangs on a dry branch
Threaten to be broken
You seem to be obsessed with
People and things
That don't belong to you
The urge to have them all

Makes you wonder
Why you are heading
Into a direction that clearly
Wasn't part of your original plan
Your life has gone astray
As you try to pick up the pieces
You can see the vultures
Hiding in human form
Hunger for the rest of your life

Feed the Hungry Ghosts
With your pure soul
They laugh at your face
While feasting on your guilt
They awake the beast inside
They control your every whim
You're their puppet
Bend over to their will

No one seems to be
What you thought they'd be
Everyone seems to have a purpose
Life changes and some of us
Cannot follow the rest
Some people turn into predators
While the rest is the easy prey
The game is on

Your slim chance is to guess
What life's supposed to be
You can only open your heart
Pray that you don't have to
Face the Hungry Ghosts
They are quite ravenous
They smell fear with an ease
Beware of the hunters
They're just around the corner

8. Soul Retriever

It's so easy to give your life
To the Soul Retriever
He's after your soul
Like a dog wants a bone
He's not the devil
He'd never be that easy
To persuaded with purity

He eats away the clear conscience
Of humanity
He leaves you bitter
He turns you into
A heartless creature without
Any remorse
Regret is foreign to him

The Soul Retriever takes
What he can get
Every opportunity
Every season
Every kind of soul
What's left behind is
An empty shell

The Soul Retriever just
Takes away your soul
He doesn't feel anything
About you
About anything
He only does what he must
He's acting on instinct
Directed by your foolish desires

Let the Soul Retriever
In your life
Is the worst option
You can take
He only finds your soul
When you attract him by
Acting like a bloody dolt
You foolishly believe

That remorse may go away
It only runs deeper
Leaving new essence to fetch
For the Soul Retriever
And this is how the story goes

9. Love is an empty word

You say you love me
I feel so lonely by it
You say you want me
My instincts tell me otherwise
You created a home
In which love is a foreigner

You act as if I'd be
Just a body to warm your bed
A shoulder to lean on
Someone you can come home to
Love is a concept lacking
In this calculation

Love is an empty word
An aid to bind me to you
To brush off your anxiety
Of my leaving your
Perfect world of control

You say you need me
You say love is holy
It must be treasured
Each day by you and me

Your eyes beg me to stay
Funny I can't recall
Any time you acted on
Those lofty words

While I do all you say
I feel like selling my soul
To the devil

10. Let me rule you

I'm the master
You're the servant
That's the rule
In the game of life
I'm the leader over you
I'm the mapmaker of your life
Your fate is in my hand
I rule the land of destiny
You have to do what I say

Just let me rule you
I'm what you need
I'm your fear
I'm your regret
I'm the man, I'm the woman
You cannot have me
But I'll always own you
I'm the lord of ancient instincts
Don't be shy
Reach out for the riches of
My destined world
Just let me rule you
And you own that world

Give me one little finger
And I swallow you up wholly
I'm the master
You never wanted
You cannot deny me
You cannot escape me
I'm above you
I'm behind you
I'm everywhere and nowhere
I'm everything and nothing

Seek me
You never find me
I'll show you the world or
Not a thing at all
You can't be rid of me
Even if you tried
Just let me rule you

11. Lost Cause

Whatever you do, don't worry
We're on the lane of the lost cause
Nothing happens without a reason
No one says it was a good one
Funny things happen, though
The laughter died down before
Still we can see a sense
In a fruitless cause
A cause that only ends up
Buried deep down in the dirt

Strange creatures cross
The lane of the lost cause
We're so much into
Their web of tales that
We cannot see where
We are heading
We're right on our way to
Our destiny

Like trusting fools
We're too blind
We cannot see any trap
In the route we're taking
No question why
Sealing our fate
By walking the lane
The lane of the lost cause

12. Autumn Leaves

Autumn Leaves reveal
Nature's retreat from summer
It's the retreat from laughter
And happiness in the sun
And the world goes still,
When the last leaf falls down
Snow is just around the corner
Everything's going silent
In the darkening of the day

Autumn Leaves prepare the
World for numbness
Dying on their way down
Shrivel up 'til nothing remains
Leaving empty trees
Letting the world know that
The darkness is coming back

Everything's fading into grey
It's not the end of the world
But the end of a cycle
The end of this life as it was
A new form of being
Is rising to tell you
All will start out new
Some day for sure

Liebe mit Fernbedienung

Ja, so eine Fernbedienung ist schon
eine tolle Sache, viele Programme,
man kann viel auswählen und jeder
kann etwas anderes sehen

Das kann ich vollkommen verstehen,
bloß wozu braucht die Liebe eine
Fernbedienung?

Als ich sagte:
"Ich liebe dich"
meinte ich
Ich liebe dich, bedingungslos, ohne Grenzen
und ohne Zweifel und Hintergedanken,
ohne ein Zeitlimit - von ganzem Herzen

Als du mir sagtest:
"Ich liebe dich"
meintest du
Hör gut zu, ich habe schon viele
Beziehungen hinter mir,
hoffentlich klappt es dieses Mal,
hoffentlich werden zusammen bleiben -
wenigstens für kurze Zeit

Ich denke, wir könnten es schaffen,
ich mag dich wirklich sehr gerne,
doch komm mir nicht zu nah

Klasse! So ist das nun in der Liebe
mit Fernbedienung, man hat das
Gleiche gewählt und sieht doch
etwas anderes!

Man sieht sich den gleichen Film an,
trotzdem hat jeder von uns
andere Details vom Film als
wichtig behalten und es fühlt
sich an wie im falschen Film zu sein

Seelenverwandte?

Seelenverwandte leben im Einklang
miteinander
Sie wissen immer, was der andere braucht,
was der andere möchte
ohne jedes Wort
Jedenfalls sagt man das so

So, eigentlich sollten wir Seelenverwandte
sein in einer einzigartigen Liebe zusammen

Der einzige kleine Schönheitsfehler
an der Sache ist,
dass wir nicht nur gleich denken
Wir reden im selben Maße um den heißen
Brei
Wir scheuen uns beide vor dem ersten Schritt
Wir machen alles andere als
zum Punkt zu kommen
Wir deuten in jeder dummen Phrase,
in jedem lächerlichen Bild, dass da mehr ist

Wir hängen in unseren Unsicherheiten fest
und verstecken uns hinter großen Worten
Wir verändern nichts dadurch
Keiner von uns traut sich
den ersten Schritt zu tun,
aus Furcht vor Zurückweisung

Nur macht das aus Seelenverwandten
zwei einsame Seelen!

English Version: Soulmates?

Soulmates have a mutual understanding
They always know what the other one needs,
what the other one wants
without saying a word -
That's what they say
So, we're supposed to be soulmates
in a unique love..

The only little mistake about this is
We're not only thinking similar
We're talking in circles in the same way
We're shying away from the first step
We're doing anything else instead of
getting to the point

We're hinting in every stupid phrase,
every silly image that there could be more
We're stuck in insecurities and hiding
behind big words

We're not changing anything with it
None of us takes the first step,
afraid of being rejected

So, these soulmates remain only
two lonely souls!

I'm trying now a positive version

Soulmates #2

My fingers still tingle from
the invisible bound between our hands
Our thoughts seem telepathic,
whenever we think of each other
the other one knows it - feels it
So, whenever we're apart
we'll never be alone,
because of the bound of our souls

We're in each other's hearts
We trust each other,
know each other
and forgive the other one's mistakes
We know, when the other one needs help
and just be there
Maybe this is planned in heaven,
maybe even a karmic thing,
I don't know,
all I know is:
I love you!

I nearly gave up believing in
heaven, believing in the good
but it came back
because of you!

and I add even more:

When I started to believe
that I only get bad things in my life
I felt the connection between
you and me
I saw your smiling face
and I felt that
I got a new hope

A hope for tomorrow,
something I lost for the longest time
With you there's a tomorrow
We're so much alike
It feels like looking into mirror
We can reach goals together;
we didn't dare to dream of alone

The healing just began,
because one soulmate feels broken
without the other soul
Unison is the key
and I know you're my home
as I can be yours
Just take my hand
and it will be true

Don't call me angel

Maybe I'm an angel in some ways, but
this little angel hides a devil beneath the
surface
Beware of its claws,
they might hurt you badly!

The devil inside of the little angel
takes you right into hell
It makes your skin crawl,
you feel its cold fear until your heart
freezes over
and the rest of you burns up in anger,
pain and agony

You want to ease the pain with alcohol
and drugs,
but what kind of hell would let
you spoil its fun of coming back in all
its purity?!
So, you suffer deep down inside,
No – don't call me angel

This little angel hides a faery inside
with its hunger for all kind of things
Its lust for life and things makes
you cross boundaries that get you into
trouble as a normal human being

It makes wanting people and things
that don't belong to you
It causes you to do mischief and pranks
at the wrong time
and hurt yourself and others by it

The faery puts on its Glamour and
you think you're in love
with a good and sweet person, but
the old trickster only fools you and
makes you do what it wants
The faery plays around and
tells you fairytales of a dreamlike living with
its magic and mystery
that will never work out in reality
No – don't call me an angel

This little angel hides an alien deep inside,
who doesn't understand this world in any sense
It talks in the same language as you, but it
does not understand you and you don't
understand it, so it will do say things the wrong way
It has no clue, how this life on earth really works
and simple things are too complicated for it
It has opinions that makes you itch
to correct its point of view
It whines about constantly feeling in the wrong place
and driving you angry and mad by it,
So, don't call me angel

Maybe – just maybe - in all of this,
there's a little left of me to love you and
care for you..
All you have to do is find me – the real me - in this chaos...

Well, then:
Tag, you're it!

Gedankenfetzen

Wichtig für Seelenpartner ist das Loslassen.
Unter normalen Umständen ist das Ganze
schon
schwer.

Doch wenn ein Seelenpartner sehr präsent ist,
egal wo der andere ist,
dann wird das Loslassen zur Lebensaufgabe.

Das wirft die Frage auf, ob es für diese
Seelenpartner Hoffnung auf eine glückliche
Liebe zusammen gibt oder ob man mitten
im Spiel aufgibt?!

Die Antwort kennt nur das Herz.

I'm a monster

You act like I am a monster,
you hide away,
you ignore me all the time,
no straight answer to the
horrible person I seem to be
Did I scare you away?

I wonder, when did I threaten you?
I always remained here and
I always stood by my word
I may seem to be confusing to you,
but I am honest to you and
I told you what was on my mind

And now I'm crying, growling,
screaming
and growing slowly into that monster...

I'm a monster #2

Welcome to my little world, where
you live in your own little world
in hurt and self destruction
Pain is the only thing you might really feel
You want to hurt yourself to feel something,
but you don't do it - at least not intentional
You hurt yourself with words

Happiness and peace only scratch the surface
and don't go down to your heart anymore
In your heart, where the love hides
behind huge walls
Nobody sees it, nobody feels it,
nobody knows it

The rest feels only numb and sad
In my world you try to smile and be good,
do the right thing - to get past
the beast that has your heart in its claws
and eats the love away till there's only pain
Yeah, you may be right

But on the way you hurt
people again and again
without the slightest clue and
storming through their lives
like a hurricane

You only realise it too late,
because you only recognise
the pain as feeling anymore
and to say I'm sorry seems
like a constant friend

The only thing that keeps you
from doing worse things is
your strength, which keeps you alive
But your strength has limits and
it's not clear how long it could last

Okay, zur Ablenkung eines Liebesgedicht

Mir schwirren tausend Worte durch den Kopf,
um Dinge zu beschreiben
Doch ich sehe dich und
weiß nicht einmal mehr meinen Namen

Ich kann es nicht beschreiben,
was ich für dich fühle
Ich kann nur fühlen
Ich weiß, es heißt Liebe,
jedoch ist mein Gefühl stärker als jedes Wort

Wenn ich an dich denke,
fallen mir tausende Dinge auf,
die ich vorher nie bemerkt hätte

Du zeigst mir Welten,
von denen ich vorher nie geträumt hätte
Du machst mir klar, dass man
Romantik nicht nur erwarten kann,
sondern dass man sie selbst fühlt

Durch dich erfahre ich,
dass ich Grenzen überschreiten kann,
du gibst mir den Mut

Jetzt weiß ich,
trotz Rückschläge, Krisen
und schlechten Zeiten,
kann ich auf gute Zeiten hoffen
und sie erleben

Du gibst mir ein Gefühl
der Geborgenheit und Rückhalt
Du gibst mir Hoffnung und Kraft

Auch wenn du es nicht wahrhaben willst,
es ist kein Traum,
mach die Augen auf,

es ist so!

Why did you walk away?

I was always here and
still I remain

You banished me from
your world
Though I never meant to intrude

I asked for permission,
but you ran away

I must be a fool,
Still waiting for you
Still hoping
you're just too shy

Still hoping that
you didn't give me up
I never give you up

I will be waiting here forever more
with open arms and never let you down,
because I love you!

Ein Zwischenspiel und ein komischer
Gedanke

Wenn die Furie der Sternschnuppe folgt,
die am Horizont langsam verglüht, wird sie
den Silberstreif am Ende der Nacht erkennen.

Der Schimmer des Lichtblicks führt sie
auf den Weg zurück zum sanften Helden

Seine warmherzige und tiefe Zuneigung
seine geduldige und leutselige Aufmerksamkeit
seine aufrichtige und zuvorkommende Wertschätzung
seine aufbauende und ruhige Kraft

Machen aus der verlorenen, erzürnten Furie wieder
die liebenswerte und großherzige Göttin von einst

Destiny

In a world full of
Suspicion, fear, envy and hatred
I tried to spread my wings
But my wings were fragile
On one day my belief was weak
I nearly gave up everything

Then I was touched
By an angel and by you
I was so happy
that tears started to run

I'm learning to
believe – really believe
that there's someone,
who's helping me to fly,
when my wings are too weak
So, I can get to higher spheres

And I know there's a soul
out there to be with me
through it all
to help and guide me
as my soul does for you

It's all destiny
meant to be by heaven

Our souls are in love,
even when we're too much
involved in other things

This love is guided by the angels
It's a "soul-love"

No one else makes me
feel this way

No one else has this
connection to me
You made me believe again

Dich gehen lassen

Ich liebe dich,
doch ich lasse dich gehen

Es bricht mir das Herz
und es schmerzt mich sehr,
doch du hast etwas Besseres verdient

Du sollst nicht dieselben Probleme
Tag für Tag erneut durchmachen
Das wäre keine Beziehung,
sondern Überlebenstraining

Ich weiß, dir geht es gut
und du bist glücklich,
da, wo du bist
und ich gönne es dir
Du hast es redlich verdient

Du hast mal gesagt
Du glaubst nicht an Engel
Für mich warst du ein Engel,
Tag für Tag, auch
wenn du es nicht weißt

Du wirst nicht mehr zurückkommen
Und das ist auch gut so

Ich würde uns beide nur zu Grunde richten
Ich wünsche dir in deinem Leben,
dass du es leben kannst wie du willst,
mit wem du willst und vor allem,
dass du es so willst!

Ich wünsche dir Liebe, Glück und Zufriedenheit
und Gesundheit und Fülle – mein Engel

Your love

Just thinking I know about you
Reading your lines
Reading the signs you sent
Seems that I was wrong
Where's your love now?

Your fine words about love
seem to be vanishing in the
light of the sun, melting away
like every daydream does

I'm no material girl,
I don't care about any "kingdom"
I'm a woman asking for your love
Just the way you are

I don't need to be
carried in your arms,
just holding me is enough
I don't need fancy cars,
I would ride on a bicycle around
the world, if you need me to

I don't give a damn about
fancy restaurants,
A dinner with just the two of us
is even more romantic
You seem to be scared
that I could expect
Something you cannot give me
Someone you aren't able to be

I'm also afraid
that you would expect that
You seem to be afraid
of the next step
Afraid of what might be
Afraid of what others may say
Afraid to change the situation
that gives you security
Afraid that you would lose too much

My fears are also making it hard
I'm afraid that you take your love away
I'm afraid that
I still wallow in self-pity
for the next years to come
I'm afraid that everything will change
I'm even more afraid that
everything remains as it was
The same dull life without your love
Expecting, waiting, fearing
to hear from you..
More than just a sign!
Only to be disappointed
at the end of each damn day
I'm tired of reading your riddles
Don't you think it's time to
be honest to me?
I think we would be perfect
for each other
Let's soothe each others fears together
and celebrate our love together
for what it is, because I don't need more

Know it all

There are times
people use to think
That I know it all
That I know about them
That I've heard it all

Not that anyone asks
only expects me to know
Not that anyone cares
Nobody wants to know,
if I really know or care
about them

Sure, it's expected to care
but not too much
that would be overstepping
an invisible line
Nobody knows that I care…

I care much
I know, it's not much worth
my care - the care of a know it all
a care of someone, who seems
to be a dreamer,
a weird one,
with no idea of the real world

Someone, who dreams to get over
her own madness can never care.
Would you care?

Expectations

I can never be the woman
you expect me to be
I can't even be the woman
I expect me to be
I remain what I am
with the hopes and fears
from long time ago
Still fighting to be
the way I am

You expect me to change
How can anything change,
if I'm still going in the same
circles and no helping hand
to get me out
I want to be there for you,
if you let me in your life

I don't expect a change of you,
you can be the way you are
you know, I can forgive many mistakes
I only don't know where to go,
who to talk to,
how to reach you

So, I'm still sitting here and
expecting just a little sign,
knowing, I will remain here forever

Strange thoughts

#1 Isn't it funny...?

Isn't it funny that I wanted to tell you: 'I love you' -
But I forgot the words very fast
Isn't it funny that I've never mentioned a single word
in my letters
Isn't it funny that I, despite my strong feelings for you,
suppress just THAT
Probably I should write to you, but I don't, because

I LOVE YOU!

#2 Flowers smell

Flowers smell, birds sing,
dogs bark, cats purr,
wolves howl - and I?

There's no pointer for me that can get
anyone's attention to me...

The secret of this magic

I thought I hold the magic wand
to enchant you,
the way you enchanted me
you smiled at me and winked at me
or so it seemed

All I could see now is the
secret of this magic,
the magic wand was just a match,
which burnt my fingers
and you only smiled and winked
at the kissing couple next to me

I know you're happy where you are
all I can I hope is
I can get happy someday where I am

Geschichte geschrieben?

Gerade wollte ich eine Geschichte schreiben,
ich machte mir die Themenauswahl nicht leicht

Ich entschied mich dafür etwas Phantastisches zu schreiben,
damit meine Träume endlich Flügel bekämen

So entstanden in meinem Geist
viele eigenartige Figuren mit sonderbaren Fähigkeiten

Jede Figur sollte ursprünglich etwas aus meinem Leben
durchmachen, nur so dramatisch war mein Leben
bisweilen nicht gewesen

So packte ich noch unmögliche Magie hinzu
und malte auch viele Bilder, um alles zu unterstreichen

Doch dann riss mein künstlerischer Faden,
jetzt suche ich jemand, der mir sagt,
wie mein Märchen endet

Nice

'You're so nice'
may sound positive,
but a dog is also nice,
sunny weather is nice,
more money is nice,
a walk in the forest is nice

Nice isn't just enough for me!

Thoughts from a fanfiction I wrote

And here I thought that I could teach you
all the things I know, because
I'm older than you

As it looks I'm none the wiser
and I have to learn many lessons
from you as well

And of course we have to learn
several things together,
so we grow together with each other
and make the best of what we have

Weird thoughts...

My mind's drifting away,
ending up in a dark mist
Good feelings and clear thoughts
are going lost in there

Someone said to me
You look like an angel
This angel is no saint,
this angel doesn't guide your way
An avenging angel,
who creates chaos
and who hurts everyone,
including herself

An angel, who prefers retreat
over taking care
The angel of destruction
destroying her own life,
destroying her own soul,
A soul that was already dead
An angel, who takes away all
your energy and happiness

I already tried to change my ways
But I always ended up at a wall
I don't have the strength anymore
to break these walls down
I'm sitting in a prison of my own
making, I'm in my own way
the only thing remained is crying
Crying for help

The only thing people hear is
the screaming of a mad woman
No, the screaming of a mad girl
that's what I remained to many

Let's be honest, I have no life
I have created a mess, inside and outside,
literally and in my mind,
and so everything's going lost in it

I've come to hate money,
it wasn't my luck, money still rules
I'm scared of the pressure on me
and the expectations of me
And everyone expects a lot of me
especially I expect a lot of myself

Funny, though the serious part in me
rules and I'm having a hard time
not jumping out of window,
there's still a spark of hope
for a wonder in me and
it makes me go on

Go on with my shallow life,
hurting myself and others,
getting more aggressive and
desperate with every second
Then again, no one takes me seriously

So, why should it matter
if I hurt someone? I can't be right,
I'm a raving mad girl

I love you, those were my words,
nobody reacted, nobody cared
Maybe I'm invisible or just
not important enough to get an answer

Nobody realises my death inside,
as long as this body and brain
work halfway as the others want me to,
why should anyone see beyond that?

Oh, I'm smiling, I can be funny,
I still have friends, sometimes
I even can be charming
everything must be alright, right?
I smile in the darkest mood and
everything I do costs a lot of
strength and will

The strength and will
I actually need to go on
One might think it's mask,
but it isn't
It helps me preventing from going
completely insane and it saves
others from my constant whining

I may see things clear,
but it doesn't make me feel better

The way to end of tunnel is too long
and I realise my life lacks
the stability of support
Not someone, who takes my hand,
and lead my way

No, just someone to be there for me,
be there with me, be on my side

I wonder if there's hope or
if anyone heard me

Did you hear me?

1. Where's..?

Where's the beauty of my soul?
Where's the kindness of my heart?
Everyone tells me I'm good person
with a beautiful soul and
a kind heart

I can't see that
I can see only the aggressions
I'm showing to everyone
who doesn't take me serious,
when I needed to be

The aggressions to all
who will not answer me,
when I need answers

The aggressions to everyone,
who expects me to be the way
they want me to
and not let be myself

And the aggressions to all people,
who are easily making me upset

The unfairness in this is that I cannot stop
the aggressions towards the wrong people
When I'm angry and helpless
I upset people, who care for me.
So, tell me, where's the beauty of my soul?

2. The other side: Another bad love poem

I love you
they're so simple words
Why can't I tell you this?
It's not that I can't form the words
or that I can't pronounce them
I just can't tell them

I'm standing here right in front of you
with wild gestures and a shy smile
and you have no clue
I know for sure,
I won't say those words
They're on the tip of my tongue,
but they won't leave my mouth...

I told you 'I love you' in my dreams,
even out loud at night,
when you weren't there
I'm a coward in this,
I can't tell you the words
I want to, so badly

I wished you would hear my thoughts
or you would get my hints,
then you would know the truth
But up to now I'm scared and
you have no clue
I can only hope, when I'm brave
enough to say those words
you won't be gone...

I'm going to get you...

I'm shy and feeling helpless
Not that you believe it
when you see me
I know you're shy, too
I have to say
I'm in love with you
and I'm going to get you

I have no clue how to do so
I did what I could,
with hinting and the letters
I wrote, but now
I'm at a point that living
with knowledge that
I'm love with you
and you might love me, too
is not enough...

I need more
I need you
I'm going to get you... somehow

I'm making a fool out of myself
again and again
but I'm going to get you

Be prepared, once I get the
idea how and the chance to do so
You'll be mine

I know there's only so much
I can do, it might seem
not so much,
but if you open your heart to me
you can see, you'll win a lot more...

I wished you could already see me,
until now you don't...
I ask you to come to me and
be with me, because
I'm in love with you
I'm going to get you..

Maybe I'm letting you get me,
the time is now and I'm free
You'll hunt me as I'm hunting you.

I'm offering you a smile
The smile that you already know
A smile I gave some time ago
Oh, yes, it was more than just
hiding... if you can read beyond it

Let's hunt each other and
believe me, each of us will win!

Patience

I've been told that patience is important
to get what I want
and to be the I want to be

Patience is a funny thing,
the first two years
it's as strong as
it has been on the first year

Then it started to fade
it came back a bit by my own force
Then some years later
I wonder what this patience is for?
What do I wait for ... still?

I did what I had to do to
get my wishes and then all I could
do is waiting patiently

I waited for you, I got no answer,
I waited for a job, I got none...
So, the patience runs out on me..
What could I wait for, the end of the world?

Then congratulations, then I won, because
my world has ended long years ago

The Beast

Heart beats fast
Claws are sharp
Fangs are bared
Wild and uncontrolled
Never go near go it
How could you love the beast?

This is how some see a wolf
but also me,
I never fit in the
role of a soft, gentle, quiet woman
I will always scream, shout, fight, cry
howl and growl, and sometimes bite
when my mood takes me
And sometimes I bark,
when I'm cornered

But a wolf can be good
and is loyal to its pack
So can I
I can be gentle, warm, friendly, lovable and
loyal to my partner, family and friends,
even doggedly so

Could love you me with the beast inside?

SINISTER

1. Some hide in the darkest corners
some let their souls die
in the cold truth of the world
Where have the dreams gone to?
All I can do is not starving, not falling down
in this harsh world without dreams

There's no release to what
I really feel and
"I love you" are only empty words
I just learn to dress myself
behind the surface of my own darkness

Chorus:

Sinister you think I am
sinister is all you can see
but this surface hides
the hurt in my soul
the pain in eyes
and it makes me sick
you can't see beyond this
It's a mask I put on
and I hide myself
(1. Putting on that mask)

2. Some cry in exhaustion of
letting their dreams die
I was giving everything
you have been asking for
The truth was always there -
but you were blinded by the light

There's no running, no hideaway
I can't change what I am
Oh - did I say "I love you"?
It sounds so empty now
Let's face the truth

Chorus

Sinister you think I am
sinister is all you can see
but this surface hides
the hurt in my soul
the pain in eyes
and it makes me sick
you can't see beyond this
It's a mask I put on
and I hide myself
(2. How I wish you could see me

Tapetenwechsel

Man redet ja sehr schnell davon,
dass jemand einen Tapetenwechsel braucht
Ich suche immer noch eine Tapete
für meine graue Seele, aber nicht dasselbe in
Grün

Menschen

Jeder Mensch trägt in sich ein Licht,
bei manchen Menschen ist es wie eine Kerze,
der erste Windstoß löscht es aus

Bei anderen ist wie ein Halogenlicht,
länger haltbar und stechend hell, aber kalt

Ich hoffe, du trägst ein Licht in dir,
das nur noch wenige in sich tragen.
warm, hell und beständig wie die Sonne

Wenn ich einmal groß bin..

Ich wollte als Kind immer groß und
schön werden und lange Haare haben

Jetzt bin ich einigermaßen groß und habe lange Haare -
nur Schönheit ist relativ

Ich wollte als Kind immer eine tolle Arbeit,
bei der ich Spaß habe
Jetzt arbeite ich nachts, um Geld zu verdienen
und das kreative Arbeiten am Computer macht mir Spaß

Ich wollte als Kind immer eine eigene Familie mit
Mann und Kindern
Jetzt kommt das eigene Kind aus der Klinik und
irgendwann vielleicht ein Partner

On Fire

Fire in your eyes was burning that night
Fire in your voice, in your words, from your mouth
It was almost burning from your skin, from your being

It was burning into my eyes,
into my ears, into me, into my senses
I was on fire,
it was raging all through me with intense heat

So, what am I supposed to do now
left alone and without your fire,
and completely burnt out?

Tell me

At first you talked
about your life - about your feelings
I was enchanted by your words
that seemed to reach me
I felt safe and accepted

Then I talked to you about my life,
about my feelings
You seemed to listen
and understand
I felt safe and accepted

You talked again about your life;
about your feelings
But there's a lack of interest in me,
I feel not safe and accepted anymore

I still got no answers from you
It hurts me to know,
you don't see me

You talk endlessly, mercilessly
about your life, about your feelings,
without asking how I feel
I feel unsure and exhausted
Tell me, is that what you wanted?

Mehr seltsame Gedanken:

Man sagt oft, dass Männer und Frauen wie Hund und
Katze sind.

In meinem Fall wäre ich allerdings die treue
und verlässliche Hündin,
die jeden als Teil ihres Rudels - ihrer Familie -
aufnimmt, akzeptiert und liebt,
auch wenn der Partner ein unabhängiger Kater ist.

Sie versucht ihr Rudel zusammenzuhalten und
lässt dem Kater seinen Freiraum,
damit er nicht nur zum Essen nach Hause kommt

Doch sollte er draußen mit anderen spielen,
wäre es angeraten sich an die Regeln zu halten,
sonst wird diese Hündin ihn anbellen oder gar beißen!

The picture of me

All you can see is the picture of me
You always see me smile
You heard my chosen words and
you think you know me

That's not all of me
I'm crying inside,
I'm dying inside,
but all you can see is the picture of me

You used to make me smile,
let me forgetting that part of me is gone
Everything inside of me is a
chaotic storm and a constant fight

But you made me smile,
though inside of me some feelings died
I only let you see the picture of me
I didn't let you see my hurt,
I didn't let you see my love,
yes, I constantly fight the love

You don't know all of me
I only let you see the picture of me

What would you do?

What would you do,
if I opened the door and let you in?
Would you be my enemy or my friend?

What would you do,
if I tell you the truth about me?
Would you run away or stay?

What would you do,
if I told you that there's much to fight?
Would you fight with me or against me?

What would you do,
if I told you to decide to be my friend or not?
Would you tell me all I need to hear
or nothing at all?

So much guesses without an answer,
then again, not answering tells also so much.

This isn't meant as blueprint for anyone, it's just
expressing my feelings, when I'm down:

Can you be my friend?

If you want to be my friend,
you have to be strong and beautiful,
because I won't be

If you keep calm and patient,
you can hold me in your arms,
when I lose control and rage madly

With warmth, listening and understanding
you can keep me from depressive thoughts
Don't fall for my big smile, it would hurt you

You need clear, gentle words to reach me,
when I break down and cry
Sometimes you need to rage with me,
When the silence is killing me,
so I can feel equal with you

If you try to keep me with you, I'll run
I don't run from you, but from myself,
so try to follow me

If you have enough courage to stay with me,
I'll show you the true love, which is
hidden in my heart and my soul
It'll give you back all the power you need
Don't wait too long, the loneliness eats me up

MY LOVE

Intro

This is like putting some old love songs together,
but this is how I feel
You know, everything returns to you some day

1) I LOVE YOU, but it's not as simple as that
You never heard my silent cry,
but right now I sing my heart out to you
You know, I'm not pretty and cute,
I'm just a woman in the crowd
Maybe you don't wanna be a prisoner of love,
I'd let you be whatever you wanna be
I can be the right one,
if you'd give me this chance

Chorus:
My love is for someone special
My love's right for you (only for you)
I can be the light that shines onto your heart and soul
You can hear me call and I'm calling your name
I'm reaching out for your love (hear me now)
I wanna hold you tight and give my love to you

2) Every time I see your face,
my heart's filled with pleasure and pain
'cause you seem so smart and so damn cool
But I've let you know, where's love to find
Don't throw it all away, before you know
You can believe in me, please, open your heart to me

More thoughts, but it could be seen
as addition to the song

Rules of my heart
that guides me to you
Rules that only let you in
Rules made for protecting you

No don'ts and dos,
Only a guidance for you
They open my heart only to you
Rules that not meant to
force, but to see the light
The rules of my heart say:

I love you,
My heart is your home..

Stille

Wenn die Einsamkeit und Stille
dich wahnsinnig machen und
dich innerlich langsam töten,
dann wird alles irrational und schwer

Ich weiß, dass du dich für mich
interessierst und mein Tun verfolgst
Manchmal teilst du meine Gedanken und
ich bin dankbar, dass du davon weißt
und damit umgehen kannst

Manchmal tut es einfach nur weh,
weil du nichts sagst oder einfach
unwissentlich über mich hinwegfegst
Du siehst mich, aber siehst nicht wie
sehr ich nach Antworten von dir lechze

Ich weiß, dass du Zeit brauchst
Leider verliere ich immer mehr
das Vertrauen, dass du irgendwann
mal deine Gedanken in Worte fasst

Irgendwann kann ich dir nicht mehr
das geben, was du brauchst,
um über dich hinauszuwachsen,
weil mir die Stille mir die Kraft raubt
und nur noch Bitterkeit übrig lässt

Farne im Wind

Ich träumte, ich sei Farne im Wind
Ein leichte Brise und es gab herrliche Abkühlung

Ein wenig stärkerer Wind und die rettenden
Regenwolken verschwanden

Der trockene, warme Fön ließ meine Blätter welken
und der tosende Sturm riss mich aus der Erde

So manches Mal geht es mir wirklich so,
ein Wind bringt die Veränderung,
ein falscher Wind jedoch
reißt mir den Boden unter den Füßen weg

Strange thoughts #1

The cage I'm in, created by my mind
stops me from getting anywhere
I go forward and get thrown back
farther away each time
I'm going blind inside, though
there are lots of images inside
It makes me weak, dumb and tired, though
I'm supposed to be clever and strong

I'm losing myself to it
Things that used to make me happy
are so dull now
Where are the feelings gone to?
I'm drowning again
I'm raging like a thunderstorm,
out of control

Is there's anything or anyone to help me?
I'm supposed to come to you,
but when I'm there you're gone
Now where's the cure to this weakness?

Strange thoughts #2

While waiting for an answer to my letters
I realised I should go to you
But I can't, I'm in my own way
The way that leads to you

Everything in me gets weaker and weaker
I can't do even simple things
I hit the wall again

Am I crazy? - Maybe!
Am I lost? - Probably!

What will I do, when I have no strength anymore?
The strength I need to survive.
I try to reach you, but I don't know how
and I haven't got the strength for it
I can only run, run away from you

Though I don't want to,
but I'm weak and my thoughts are chaotic

I die inside, surviving as empty shell
and hitting the wall over and over again

There's no one to hold on to for me
I'm drowning in my chaos, leaving a mess behind

My universe is in chaos, because I don't know
why I should keep anything in Order for no one

Weaker and weaker, leaving me dumb and dull
I don't know, what to write anymore
Things and people I loved are not important anymore
No will to live

A nice wish for a plastic surgery came to mind,
but then a stranger would look into my mirror
with the same weird thoughts,
so I need a brainwash from these horrible thoughts

Looking at myself, telling myself it's okay
and waiting for an answer...

Strange thoughts #3

Letters, I wrote to you without a care
you turned away and won't let me in
that is all I know
these are the last grasps of sanity
it all comes down on me in insanity

I'm so dumb now,
I didn't feel the car crash into the wall
I shouldn't have driven anyway
I feel things dying surround me and inside me
Inside me it dies faster than it should

I'm older outside, without being wise
being dumb, silly, tired and weak
drowning me more and more
Is there a key?
Who knows? And who cares? Do I care?
I don't know - it feels only numb.

Is there a reason to care?
I don't know my life's going in circles.
Is there a way out of this Labyrinth?

Maybe, but the way I'm on is under water
and no one told me how to swim
If there's life out there that's meant to be for me,
so, please tell me...

Barfuß

Ich gehe barfuß über Pflasterstein,
das ist hart und meist sogar kantig

Ich gehe barfuß über Rasen,
ein wenig weicher, aber dumpf

Ich gehe barfuß über Moos,
das ist weich und federnd

So ähnlich ist es im Leben;
Mal hart und kantig; mal ein wenig weicher,
aber auch mal dumpf, weich und federnd

Der alte Baum

Der alte Baum hat im Park hat schon vieles erlebt
Als Kind spielte ich unter seinem Blätterkranz

Seine Rinde trägt schon viele Narben,
viele Verliebte haben schon ihre Namen darin
eingeritzt

Der alte Baum spendet mir Schatten,
wenn die Sonne gleißend auf die Erde scheint

Seine Krone ist die Heimat von Insekten,
Eichhörnchen und Vögeln

Dieser ganze Trubel machte ihm nicht so viel aus,
aber was ist in 50 Jahren?
Wird es dann noch
den Park mit dem alten Baum geben?

Geradeaus?

Jeder Mensch sollte gerade, klare Gedanken haben
Es ist zu komisch, bei mir haben die Gedanken
ständig Kurven, Kreuzungen und Verknüpfungen,
Sackgassen, verborgene Türen, steile Wände,
Falltüren, Hintertüren, Geheimgänge und
Hindernisse, die manchmal unüberwindbar scheinen

In meiner Realität ist es noch nie geradeaus gegangen,
da wo es bei anderen in geordneten Bahnen läuft,
herrscht bei mir Chaos

Manchmal kann ich nicht mal
den Silberstreif am Horizont sehen und
frage mich wozu
Wozu noch aufstehen und durchschlagen?

Manchmal ist der einzige Grund nur der,
auf den richtigen Zeitpunkt zu warten und
dann kann ich weiterkämpfen

Sichtweisen

Ich gehe durch die Stadt und überlege,
was andere in mir sehen

Die Leute kommen mir entgegen
und beschäftigen sich mit Ihren Problemen,
doch jeder mustert den anderen

Wenn sich einmal ein unerwarteter Blick trifft,
scheinen sich Rivalen gegenüber zu sein,
weil alles Mögliche da hinein interpretiert wird

Erst ein weiterer Blick kann es manchmal aufklären
Einige Schritte weiter ist man froh über die netten
Leute, die man in der Stadt sah

Gemein

Wer kennt das nicht,
jemanden passiert etwas Ungeschicktes
und man muss plötzlich lachen

Aber man sollte sich mal überlegen,
man ist die Person, der das passiert,
dann ist kein Anzeichen von Lachen zu
bemerken

Plötzlich ist die ach so kleine Welt wieder
riesengroß
und der Abstand zu unfairen Menschen ist
sehr weit
Man ist ja nicht so...
Man bleibt auf dem Teppich seiner
Möglichkeiten!

Nie würde man einer anderen Person in so
einer Situation das antun!

Ha- Ha- Ha!

Licht im Herzen

Weißt du nicht, dass ich nur für
dich ein Licht im Herzen trage?

Wenn du nicht mehr bist
wird es nicht verlöschen, sondern
lediglich die Intensität ändern

Nichts konnte es bislang
erschüttern:
Keine Trennung, Schmerz
oder Schweigen oder Vergessen
Nicht einmal der Zahn der Zeit

Auch wenn du es
nicht sehen kannst,
kannst du es trotzdem spüren,
wenn du mich lässt

Sag mir, soll ich dir das Licht zeigen?

Die Liebe siegt?

Die Liebe ist das
stärkste Gefühl
und die stärkste
Macht, die wir hier
auf Erden haben

Ich schrieb dir
eins ums andere Mal
Ich liebe dich,
doch du warst taub

Ich habe dir
in den schönsten Farben
ausgemalt wie die
Liebe in mir aussieht,
doch du warst farben-blind

Ich zeigte dir
die Gefühle in meinem
Herzen, die mit dem
Wort Liebe kaum
angerissen werden,
doch du warst unberührbar

Ich habe auf
dich gewartet,
falls du Zeit gebraucht
hättest, um
deinen Mut zusammen
zu nehmen oder um
nachzudenken,
aber du versteckst
dich immer noch

Die Liebe siegt,
das war mein letzter Gedanke,
nun ist es vorbei,
ich mag nicht mehr,
ich kann nicht mehr;
fühlen und denken

Was nützt einem die
Macht der Liebe, wenn
man es mit Gefühlskälte
zu tun hat?!

Magie

Bevor ich dich sah, da glaubte ich an Nichts
Ich war von Nichts zu beeindrucken

Niemand konnte sich in meiner Seele spiegeln
und mein Herz gehörte mir

Du hast die Magie in dir,
mit der du meine Welt verzauberst

Dein Zauber ist der Weg zu meinem Herzen

Du zeigst mir die Liebe darin,
damit ich sie dir wiedergebe

Liebe ist nur schön, wenn man sie teilen kann

Liebe ist der einzig wahre Zauber,
der Herzen öffnen kann

Einsam

Es ist ein schöner Tag draußen,
die Sonne scheint,
in jedem werden die Frühlingsgefühle geweckt

Ich sitze hier alleine in diesem kalten,
halb dunklen Raum
und mache mir nur Gedanken darüber
wie ich dich erreiche

Draußen laufen viele Leute in T-Shirts herum,
aber ich würde mich am liebsten
hinter dem dicksten Schal verstecken

Die Einsamkeit ist so ein eisiges Gefühl,
dass meine Seele bald zufriert

Das schöne Leben

In der Schule hatte ich keine Freunde
und die Lehrer erklärten mir,
ich hätte ein schönes Leben
Alles lief immer mehr aus dem Ruder

Ich war in der Psychiatrie,
dort sagten mir die Ärzte
welch' schönes Leben ich hätte

Ich leihe mir von meinen Eltern mehrere tausend Euro,
um den Start in ein schönes Leben zu schaffen

Nun habe ich kein Geld, keinen Plan, keinen Freund
und warte alleine auf das schöne Leben...

Ich sitze weinend in meinem Zimmer
und meine Welt im Inneren zerbricht,
meine Mutter kommt herein
und erzählt mir wie schön doch mein Leben ist!

Ein Tag

Es regnet schon den ganzen Tag lang,
so dass viele depressiv davon werden
Ein Gewitter zieht über unser Haus hinweg,
es färbt den Himmel gelb-grau

Ich öffne die Vordertür und atme den Duft des Regens,
voller Begeisterung sitze ich auf der Stufe im Türrahmen
Ich beobachte das Naturschauspiel
und mache mir dabei verzückt
die schönsten Gedanken

Jemand sagt mir, ich solle die Tür schließen,
bei diesem Wetter würde man
keinen Hund nach draußen schicken

Ich lächele nur und schaue wieder raus,
die Wolken klären sich auf
und durch die Sonnenstrahlen entsteht ein Regenbogen

Es regnet immer noch
und ich rase mit meinen weißen Socken nach draußen,
voller Freude tanze auf der Straße

Ich glaube, nur so kann man einen Regentag
überstehen...

Regeln in dieser Welt

Um mit anderen in dieser Welt zu leben
gibt es einige Regeln für das Zusammenleben

Einige dieser Regeln sind Klischees, an denen
man sich nicht orientieren muss,
aber es gerne tut, weil einfacher ist

Natürlich sind Männer und Frauen verschieden,
aber ein paar Unterschiede sind nicht so
gravierend wie es dargestellt wird
und oft sind wir uns ähnlicher als wir glauben
und manchmal verschwimmen die Grenzen

Also, einfach mal die Messlatte neu anlegen
und jeden so lassen wie er ist

Nur vieles was das Zusammenleben betrifft,
begründet sich in der Vergangenheit
und die prägt nun mal das Jetzt,
doch kann man seine Vergangenheit nicht ändern,
sondern nur mit seiner Zukunft leben.

The silent one

You think that I don't know you,
but actually I know you better than anyone else
I can see so many details of your life
that others seem to ignore

It makes me think of you and me
In some way we're so different
as winter and spring
On the other hand we're so similar
that I feel like looking into mirror

I smile with you, I cry with you
and I even rage with you,
but I do it on my own - all alone

With you I'm at a loss for words,
sometimes because it's only sympathy
sometimes because you impressed me
sometimes because you drive nuts with insanity
sometimes because I feel with you deeply

Is it fascination or more - like companionship?
Is it friendship or even love?
I honestly have no clue!
As long as I can't sort it out for myself,
I cannot tell you how I feel about you

A male soul cries

I'm standing here as a lonely man
touched by the cold silence
You left me behind
I try to understand
what happened to paradise
and paradise was with you
You said your love will never die
So, why am I here alone?
You said I'm too blind to see

Chorus:
Your love is all I need in my life
Where has the love gone to?
My soul yearns my for its mate
I'm not the man you can see

The strength is a pretended one
My sharp tongue, my wit
and my sarcasm are weapons
to remain aloof

So you cannot see the
hurt and grief in me
I wanted it all
I wanted the world
I come to understand
that you're my world
Even if you never know,
I love you
It's all I have and
It's all I need

Now I stand here on my own again
But it seems that
you cannot see me as well

For I long for you
You promised me
all the love you have
but why do I feel empty now?

Open your eyes and see
that I still wait for you here

I cannot promise you
open arms and a big Hello,
but for you

I try to be a better man
every day of my life

Am Glück vorbei?

Eigentlich ist es schön, wenn jemand auf subtile Weise
einem zu zeigen versucht, dass man Interesse an ihm
hat, ohne jemanden auf die Füße zu treten
Kleine Gesten, ein feines Lächeln, liebevolle Worte
sind
Balsam für zerbrechliche Seelen
Die Holzhammermethode ist etwas für Doofe,
die nicht zwischen den Zeilen lesen können -
so dachte ich

Zu spät merkte ich, dass du etwas von mir wolltest
Wer bin ich denn schon?
Es gibt attraktivere und bessere Frauen als ich es bin,
also, warum solltest du ausgerechnet mich meinen?!
Du hast von dem Glitzern in den Augen geredet,
das vom Lächeln kommt
Auch dabei kannst du mich nicht meinen,
denn mein Lächeln reicht schon lange nicht mehr
bis zu den Augen

Zu spät realisierte ich, dass du mir bereits Vertrauen
entgegen gebracht hast und dich in Krisenzeiten
auf mich verlassen hast, denn ich bin immer da
Leider waren andere auch für dich da, also
gab es keinen Grund für dich auf jemanden mit
wirren Gedanken zurückzugreifen

Das Leben ist voller Überraschungen und
Verwirrungen und einige Sachen sind einfach zu
komplex und subtil, um sie zu sehen
Und jetzt ist der Zug wohl abgefahren, weil
ich zu blind war deine Signale wahrzunehmen

Ich bin immer noch da,
um dir Schutz zu geben, wenn du ihn benötigst
um dich zu leiten, wenn du es brauchst
um dich zu lieben, wenn du es willst
um dir die Freiheit zu geben du selbst zu sein!

Ich weiß, dass du auch Probleme hast Vertrauen
zu fassen, dafür bist du zu oft hintergangen, ausgenutzt,
verletzt und enttäuscht worden

Leider kann ich dir nicht versprechen, dich nicht auch
hin oder wieder zu verletzen oder zu enttäuschen -
dafür sind wir nun mal Menschen, die nicht perfekt sind
Aber ich bin jemand, auf den du dich verlassen kannst

Falls du es noch mal versuchen möchtest, solltest du doch wohl
einen sanften, liebevollen und netten, metaphorischen
Holzhammer herausholen, damit ich weiß, dass du mich meinst

Wenn du das Glitzern in meinen Augen vermisst, dann mach dir
eines klar: Du bist es, der ein wahres Lächeln auf mein Gesicht
zaubert!
Bis dahin bin ich hier!

Danksagung

Vielen Dank an alle, die mich inspiriert haben,
bewusst oder unbewusst, positiv wie negativ,
erzwungen oder nicht, ich danke Euch von Herzen

Danke an die Leute, die sich bis zur letzten Seite
durch meine wirren Gedanken gekämpft haben,
leider muss ich Euch sagen, ihr gewinnt keinen
Blumentopf dafür, aber ab und zu ein kleines
Lächeln!

Und vielleicht kann ich Euch auch damit
in irgendeiner Weise inspirieren und wenn es nur
damit ist, dass ihr euch sagt, ihr könnt das besser
als die Alte und verschwendet nicht so viel Papier
mit Quatsch - na denn, viel Glück!

Zum Schluss noch vielen Dank an meine Familie
und meine Freunde, auch wenn man sich nicht immer
versteht, wir können trotzdem zusammenhalten.

Alles Liebe und Gute Euch allen!

Eure Astrid